Disney PRINCESS

CELEBRATE with Ariel

Plan a *Little Mermaid* Party

Niki Ahrens

Lerner Publications ◆ Minneapolis

To Eloise, Tecolote treasure

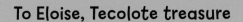

Lerner Publications Company
An imprint of Lerner Publishing Group, Inc.
241 First Avenue North
Minneapolis, MN 55401 USA

For reading levels and more information, look up this title at www.lernerbooks.com.

Main body text set in Billy Infant.
Typeface provided by Sparky Type.

Library of Congress Cataloging-in-Publication Data

Names: Ahrens, Niki, 1979- author.
Title: Celebrate with Ariel : plan a Little Mermaid party / Niki Ahrens.
Description: Minneapolis, MN, USA : Lerner Publications, [2020] | Series: Disney
    princess celebrations | Includes bibliographical references and index.
Identifiers: LCCN 2019011419 (print) | LCCN 2019014074 (ebook) |
    ISBN 9781541582743 (eb pdf) | ISBN 9781541572713 (lib. : alk. paper)
Subjects: LCSH: Party decorations—Juvenile literature. | Children's parties—
    Juvenile literature. | Little mermaid (Motion picture : 1989)
Classification: LCC TT900.P3 (ebook) | LCC TT900.P3 .A43 2020 (print) |
    DDC 745.594/1—dc23

LC record available at https://lccn.loc.gov/2019011419

Manufactured in the United States of America
1-46538-47583-7/12/2019

Table of Contents

A Wonder-Filled Party

Ariel's curiosity leads her to an exciting new world full of wonder.
Start planning a wonder-filled party! Here's what you'll need to do:

- Ask a parent or guardian for permission to throw your *Little Mermaid* party and for help in choosing a time and place. Then send your invitations!

- Create undersea wonder with decorations, party favors, and your treat menu. Clean your party place too.

- Lead guests in fun party activities!

- When the party is over, clean up the space and send thank-you cards.

Party Host Tips

- Be a kind host, and think about your guests' food allergies when planning your party menu.

- Take care of your party project workspace by covering it with newspaper.

- Stay safe when handling food. Wash your hands before making treats, and ask an adult for help when using the oven.

- Show respect by including and thanking every guest.

- Treasure Earth. Clean up and recycle all the materials you can after the party.

Oyster Invitations

Oysters are just one of many sea creatures living in the kingdom of Atlantica. Send out inviting oysters that hold pearly surprises.

Materials

• paper plates

• craft glue

• cotton balls or pom-poms

• pen

• watercolor paint and paintbrush or markers

1. Fold the paper plate in half.

2. Glue a cotton ball or pom-pom pearl inside the plate near the middle just below the fold line.

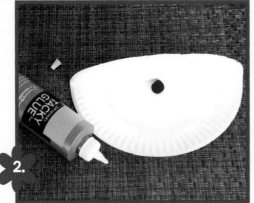

3. Write your invitation inside your oyster shell. Be sure to include any special instructions for your party as well as your party date, time, and place!

4. Decorate the outside of your oyster shell with paint or markers.

5. Send an invitation to each guest!

Party Tip! Did You Know?

A pearl forms when an oyster or other shelled sea creature covers an item, such as a grain of sand, with hard, shiny material. Oyster pearls are much more common than pearls from other creatures such as clams.

Fish Decorations

Surround your guests with dazzling ocean
wonders with these fun, fishy decorations.

Materials

• bright paper muffin
  liners

• scissors

• glue stick

• googly eyes

• crayons

• painter's tape

1. Flatten a muffin liner. Fold it in half, lining up the curves of the circle.

2. Fold the liner in half once more to make a triangle with one rounded side.

3. Unfold the liner, and cut along the fold lines, making four pieces of equal size.

4. Flatten a new muffin liner. Glue one of the pieces you cut out in step 3 to the back of the new muffin liner.

5. Glue a googly eye to the muffin liner on the side opposite the tail. Use a crayon to draw on a fishy smile below the eye.

6. Make as many vibrant fish as you'd like. Create a colorful ocean scene by taping them around your party space!

Party Tip! Be Earth-Friendly

Cut ocean bubbles from muffin liner scraps, and add them to your undersea scene. You can find other recycled objects to help decorate your space too. Bubble packaging would make fun bubbles!

Sebastian Table Toppers

Sebastian is a loyal friend who watches over Ariel. Decorate your party table with a crafted crab.

Materials

- scissors

- cardboard egg carton

- red tempera paint

- medium-size paintbrush

- red pipe cleaner

- pushpin

- craft glue

- 2 googly eyes

- black marker

1. Cut one cup from the egg carton.

2. Paint the outside of the cup red, and allow it to dry.

3. Cut the pipe cleaner into 6 even pieces.

4. Carefully use the pushpin to poke 2 holes about 0.25 inches (0.6 cm) apart into the center of the cup's flat bottom.

5. Poke one piece of pipe cleaner into each hole so that most of the pipe cleaner is sticking out the top.

6. Glue a googly eye to the end of each of the pipe cleaners you just added. Draw Sebastian's mouth on the front of the cup with the black marker.

7. Use the remaining 4 pipe cleaner pieces to make 2 Y shapes by twisting the end of 1 piece onto the center of another.

8. Use the pushpin to poke holes into opposite sides of the egg-cup body. Push the bottoms of the Y shapes into the holes.

9. Decorate your party space with your new friend!

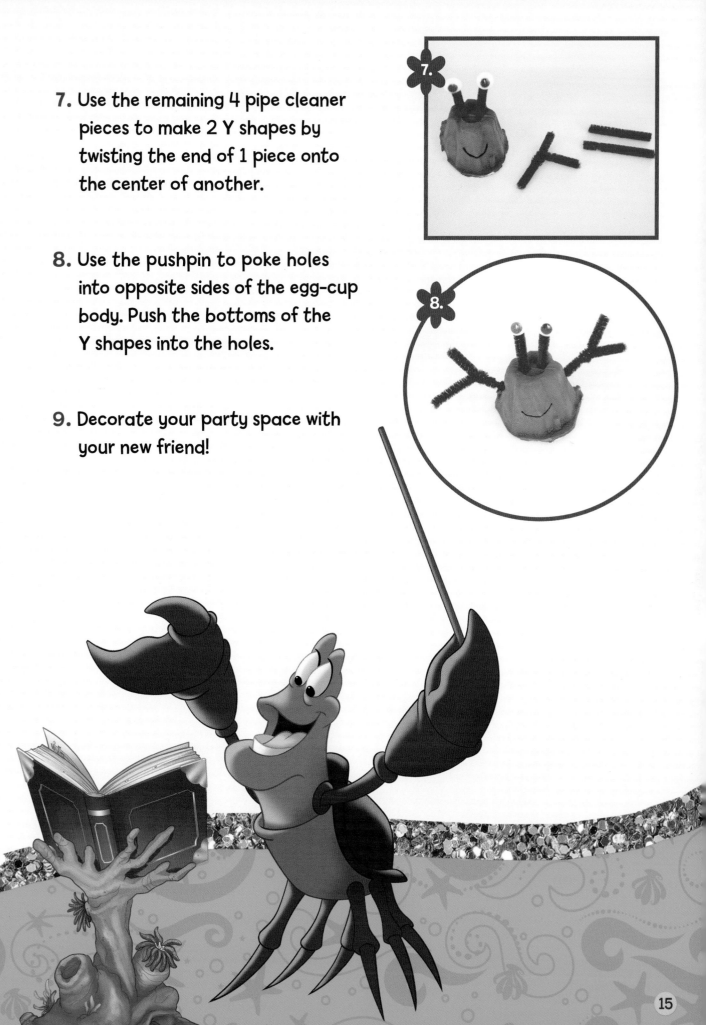

Mermaid Tail Treats

Ariel's mermaid tail helps her swim through the sea. Serve colorful treats shaped like mermaid tails. Yum!

Materials

- sharp knife

- cutting board

- round pizza pan

- butter knife

- pizza cutter

- plates

Ingredients

This recipe serves 8.

- 1 to 2 apples

- 2 cups berries

- 16 ounces (454 g) refrigerated sugar cookie dough

- 1 cup vanilla frosting

1. Wash your hands and rinse the fruit. Ask an adult to use a sharp knife to cut your apples into thin wedges. If you use berries that need to be cut, ask an adult to cut them.

2. Spread the dough into one big circle on the pan. Ask for an adult's help to bake the dough as instructed on its package.

3. When the cookie dough is finished baking, ask an adult to remove it from the oven and let the cookie cool.

4. Use a butter knife to spread frosting evenly across the cookie.

5. Top the frosted cookie with sliced berries.

6. Ask an adult to use the pizza cutter to cut the cookie into triangular slices. Move the slices to plates.

7. Add two apple wedges to the inside point of each slice for a fish tail.

Party Tip! Did You Know?
Cultures around the world have different stories about sea creatures. In Japan, there are stories of a giant fish with a human face. Ireland has legends of mermaids called *merrows*.

Mystery Treasures Game

Ariel loves collecting objects from the human world. She keeps these treasures safe in a secret spot. Play a musical guessing game with treasures that your guests bring!

Materials

- 1 special object for each person

- 1 paper bag for each object

- music player and music

1. Before your party, ask guests to bring a special object, such as a small toy or knickknack, inside a closed paper bag labeled with their name.

2. During the party, invite guests to sit in a circle with their closed bags.

3. Start the music and pass the closed bags around the circle. Ask an adult to stop the music at a random time.

4. When the music stops, players will hold onto the bag in their hands. If any players are holding the bag that they brought to the party, keep passing until everyone is holding a new bag.

5. Invite your guests to reach into their bags and feel the mystery objects inside. No peeking!

6. Players will take turns guessing what is inside the bag they're holding.

7. After a player guesses, the treasure's owner will tell everyone if the player was right or wrong. If the player was right, put the treasure in the circle's center. If the player was incorrect, the item stays in the bag.

8. After everybody has had a chance to guess, start the music again and pass the remaining bags that still have mystery treasures. Repeat steps 4 to 7.

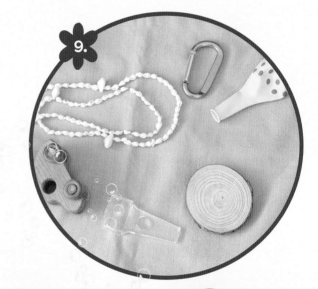

9. Continue playing until every treasure is in the center!

Party Tip! Be Respectful

Prepare extra mystery bags for guests who don't bring one. Include each guest and mystery bag in the game. And remember to return your friends' treasures to them when the game is over.

Sea Bubbles Party Favors

Life under the sea just wouldn't be the same without bubbles. Send bubble party favors home with your guests.

Materials

- 2 cups water

- ⅓ cup dish soap

- 1 teaspoon glycerin

- mixing bowl with a spout

- spoon

- 1 mini jar and lid for each guest

- pen

- blank sticker labels (one for each jar)

- clear tape

- 1 straw for each jar

1. Pour the water, dish soap, and glycerin into the mixing bowl, and gently mix with a spoon to create a bubble solution.

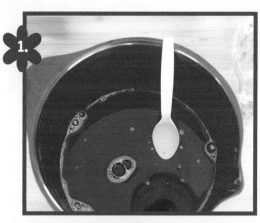

2. Pour the bubble solution into mini jars. Close the lids tightly.

3. Write "bubbles" on the blank sticker labels. Stick the labels to the jars.

4. Tape a straw to each jar lid to use as a bubble wand. Guests can dip the straw's end in the solution and blow through the other end to create bubbles.

Flounder Thank-You Cards

Ariel is grateful for her friend Flounder. Send your guests Flounder cards to show how grateful you are that they came to your party.

Materials

- construction paper

- crayons

1. Fold the construction paper in half, matching its shorter sides, to make a card.

2. Open the card like a book. Draw a heart using the fold line as the heart's center. Leave 1 to 2 inches (2.5 to 5 cm) of space between the outside of the heart and the outer edges of the paper.

3. Turn the heart sideways. Draw a triangular tail on the heart's point.

4. Draw Flounder's nose on the opposite side of the heart from the tail, just below the fold line. Make a sideways fishhook shape starting from the center of the heart and looping up toward the fold line.

5. Add a big smile below the nose.

6. Draw two eyes and eyebrows above the nose and mouth.

7. Add fins and stripes to Flounder, and decorate the rest of the card.

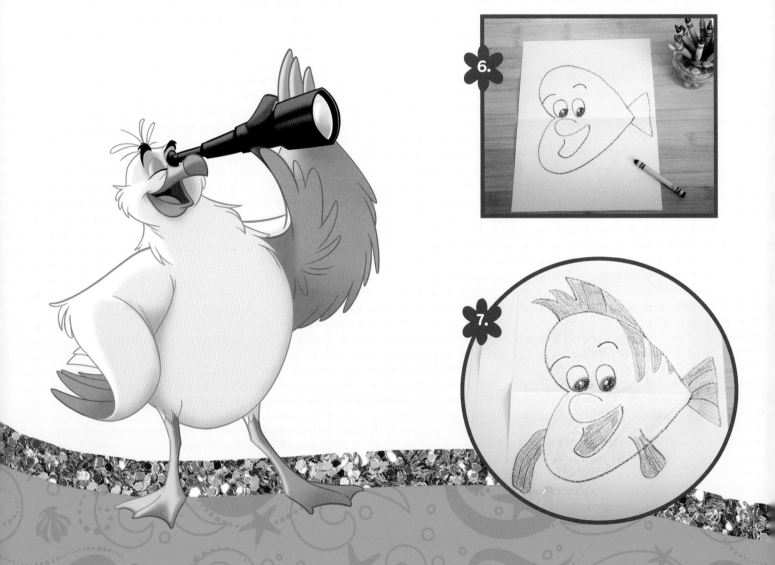

8. On the back of the paper, write a thank-you note to your guest.

9. Send a card to each guest!

Celebrate What You Treasure

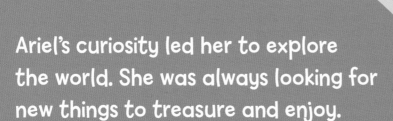

Ariel's curiosity led her to explore the world. She was always looking for new things to treasure and enjoy.

How can you plan a party that celebrates your spirit and what you treasure? Be inspired by Ariel's sense of adventure as you plan party ideas that bring you wonder and joy!

Glossary

curiosity: a wish to know more about something

guest: someone who attends a person's event or party

host: a person who holds an event or party for guests

legend: a story from the past

loyal: faithful to something or someone

oyster: a sea creature with a rough, uneven shell in two hinged parts

spout: narrow opening for pouring

vibrant: bright

To Learn More

BOOKS

Boothroyd, Jennifer. *Disney Princess Quizzes: From Ariel to Tiana*. Minneapolis: Lerner Publications, 2020. Learn more about your favorite Disney princesses.

Felix, Rebecca. *Mini Decorating.* Minneapolis: Lerner Publications, 2017. Decorate party spaces big and small with this mini decorating guide.

WEBSITES

Ariel: Explore New Worlds
https://princess.disney.com/ariel
Explore fun games, activities, and videos all about Ariel.

We Want to Give Flounder a Hug
https://ohmy.disney.com/news/2013/05/13/we-want-to-give
-flounder-a-hug/
Enjoy some of Flounder's most special moments.

Index

PHOTO CREDITS

Additional photos: art_of_sun/Shutterstock.com, p. 2; Julia Sudnitskaya/
Shutterstock.com, p. 3; Nong Mars/Shutterstock.com, p. 5T; spass/Shutterstock.com,
p. 5B; Victoria 1/Shutterstock.com, p. 7T; wavebreakmedia/Shutterstock.com,
p. 7B. Cover and design elements: Susii/Shutterstock.com (balloons); YamabikaY/
Shutterstock.com (glitter); surachet khamsuk/Shutterstock.com (glitter).